The junk drawer is one of my favorite off-limits places.

It's like a pirate treasure chest.

Only with no rubies.

I opened the drawer.

I looked inside.

Wow, I thought. *This drawer is full of cool stuff!*

And that's when all my trouble started.

ROSCOE RILEY

Rules

#1

Never Glue Your Friends to Chairs

Katherine Applegate
illustrated by Brian Biggs

HarperTrophy®
An Imprint of HarperCollinsPublishers

For Julia and Jake, with love

Harper Trophy® is a registered trademark of
HarperCollins Publishers
Roscoe Riley Rules #1: Never Glue Your Friends
to Chairs
Text copyright © 2008 by Katherine Applegate
Illustrations copyright © 2008 by Brian Biggs

Library of Congress Cataloging-in-Publication Data
is available.
ISBN 978-0-06-114882-8 (trade bdg.)
ISBN 978-0-06-114881-1 (pbk.)

Typography by Jennifer Heuer
13 CG/OPM 20 19 18 17 16 15 14 13

First Edition

Never Glue Your
Friends to Chairs

Contents

1

Welcome to Time-Out

Hey! Over here!

It's me. Roscoe.

Welcome to the Official Roscoe Riley Time-out Corner.

Want to hang out with me?

I have to warn you, though. We're going to be here for a while.

See, I kinda got in some trouble today. Again.

Kids have to follow so many rules!

Sometimes my brain forgets to remember them all.

It's not like I *try* to find ways to get in trouble. It's just that trouble has a way of finding me.

Truth is, I'm just a normal, everyday kid like you.

My favorite food is blue M&M's. My favorite sport is bed jumping. My favorite color is rainbow.

And my most not-favorite thing is lima beans.

See? Like I said. Just a normal, everyday kid.

A normal, everyday kid who sometimes gets into trouble.

Like today. I was just trying to help out my teacher.

How was I supposed to know you shouldn't glue people to chairs?

With Super-Mega-Gonzo Glue?

You've done that, haven't you?

Oh.

Never?

Oh.

Well, maybe you should hear the whole story. . . .

2

Something You Should Know
Before We Get Started

Here's the thing about Super-Mega-Gonzo
Glue.

When the label says *permanent*, they
mean permanent.

As in FOREVER AND EVER.

3

Something Else You Should Know
Before We Get Started

You gotta trust me on this.

Super-Mega-Gonzo Glue is for gluing
THINGS.

Not PEOPLE.

It is a way bad idea to glue THINGS to
PEOPLE.

That's just a for-instance.

4

This Morning at My House

You're probably wondering how I know so much about Super-Mega-Gonzo Glue.

Well, it all started this morning. I was helping my mom pack my lunch.

"Banana?" I asked her. "With no icky brown spots on it?"

Mom looked in my lunch box.

"Check," she said.

"Little fishy crackers?"

"Check."

"Gigantic chocolate cupcake with tons of gooey frosting and those little sprinkle things?"

Mom smiled her I'm-getting-tired-of-this smile.

"Sorry," she said. "We're fresh out of gigantic chocolate cupcakes."

I sighed. "It was worth a try."

Mom grabbed a comb off the kitchen counter. "Hair time, buddy. You want to look extra handsome for the open house."

In the afternoon, all the parents were coming to visit our classroom.

That's called an open house.

Even though it's at school.

We were going to sing a song about bees.

And have desserts and juice and milk.

I was especially excited about the dessert part.

My mom was bringing her banana-avocado-raisin cream pie.

I was not so excited about that.

My mom is a great mom.

But she is not a great cook.

"You have to be extra nice to Ms. Diz," I said.

Ms. Diz is my first-grade teacher. She is brand-new.

She loves teaching my class. Even though we get a little crazy sometimes.

Ms. Diz says we are very high-spirited.

"Of course we'll be nice," Mom said.

"'Cause this is her first time showing us off. And also 'cause the principal will be there."

"I promise Dad and I will behave," Mom said.

"And be sure to clap after we do our bee song," I added.

"I promise," Mom said.

"And no laughing," I added.

"Why would we laugh, sweetheart?"

"Because yesterday when we practiced it was kind of a mess," I said. "The head bobbles kept coming off."

Mom frowned and asked, "What's a head bobble?"

"You know. The ten knees on a bee head?"

I put my hands on my head and wiggled my pointer fingers to show her.

"Oh." Mom smiled. "You mean the *antennae*."

"I'm lucky. 'Cause I'm in the rhythm

section. We pound with sticks to keep the beat. And we get bobbles too."

"That's a very important job." Mom kissed the top of my head. "Don't worry. I'm sure everything will go perfectly today."

Mom zipped up my lunch box. "Okay, kiddo. You're good to go."

Just then I remembered something.

"Wait!" I cried. "There is one more really important thing! I was supposed to bring art supplies yesterday. For the art cupboard. 'Member? You said we would bring them 'cause it's easier than being a room mother?"

"Oops. I almost forgot," said Mom. She grinned. "Roscoe to the rescue!"

My family likes to say that when I help out.

My dad came in and poured a cup of coffee.

He was wearing a business suit, a brown sock, and a bare foot.

"Morning," he said. "Roscoe, is your brother up yet?"

"Yep," I said. "But I had to use my Roscoe Riley Sneak Attack to wake him. Would you like to try it sometime?"

"I'm listening," Dad said.

He made one eyebrow go up.

It's a trick a lot of dads can do.

"Well, first you knock real polite on Max's door. Then he growls and tells you to come back next year."

"And then?" asked Dad.

"Then you jump on his bed like it's a trampoline. And you scream, 'RISE AND SHINE, YOU BUM!' And if he still doesn't

wake up, you squirt him with your juice box on his nose and toes."

"I see," said Dad. "Crude, but effective."

It is always nice when your dad is proud of you.

"Mom," I said. "What about the art stuff?"

Mom was using the toaster for a mirror. "I have bags under my eyes," she said.

I tugged on her sleeve.

Sometimes that helps moms focus.

"Mom," I said. "We need goo sticks and scissors and paper."

"*Glue* sticks," Mom said. "The art supplies are in the junk drawer. Would you get them, Roscoe? I need to see if Max is ready for school."

The junk drawer is one of my favorite off-limits places.

It's like a pirate treasure chest.

Only with no rubies.

I opened the drawer.

I looked inside.

Wow, I thought. *This drawer is full of cool stuff!*

And that's when all my trouble started.

5

Don't-You-Dare Glue

The junk drawer always has wonderful things in it.

Keys. Puzzle pieces. Paper clips. The head from one of Hazel's dolls.

I was playing brain surgeon the day that happened.

The patient died.

I pulled out the bag of art supplies.

I added three purple rubber bands to the bag.

And a Slinky that wouldn't slink anymore.

And the doll head.

You never know when you might need an extra head.

And then I saw something else in the drawer.

A bottle of Super-Mega-Gonzo Glue.

The grown-up glue Mom calls *don't-you-dare* glue.

Super-Mega-Gonzo Glue is extra strong.

Dad used it when I broke my great-grandma's very old teacup.

And when I broke Mom's very precious flower vase.

And when I broke Grandpa's very ugly glass potato souvenir from Idaho.

Adults really should keep breakable stuff away from us kids.

Mom glanced into the family room. "Max! Did you find your other shoe? The bus will be here in five minutes."

My big brother came into the kitchen.

He was armed with a juice box.

"My shoe is on the roof," Max said. Then he squirted me with his straw.

At least it was apple juice. That's my favorite.

"Max!" Mom cried.

"He started this war," Max said.

"My hair's all wet," I complained.

"Maybe you should cut off your head," Max said.

Which was not all that helpful, really.

"Shut up," I said to Max.

"Roscoe!" Dad said.

"Shut up, PLEASE," I said.

"Wait just a minute, Max," Mom said. "Did you say your shoe is *on the roof*?"

"There's a good explanation," Max said.

"I'm sure there is," said Dad. His eyebrow went up again.

That eyebrow gets a lot of exercise.

"Me and Roscoe were playing astronaut," Max said.

"Max's shoe was the space shuttle," I added.

"I need a ladder," Mom said.

"I need more coffee," Dad said.

"I need a new brother," I said.

"You need a new brain," said Max.

"Guys," said Dad. "Peace."

"Roscoe, Max and your dad and I have work to do on the roof," Mom said. "Keep an eye on Hazel for me, sweetie."

Hazel is my little sister. She was busy watching cartoons in the family room.

Mom says educational cartoons are okay.

Especially until she's had her first cup of coffee.

"I'll hold the ladder," Dad said to Mom, "if you climb."

Dad is afraid of heights. But don't tell anybody. It's a family secret.

Also, please don't tell him he is losing his hair.

Dads can be very sensitive, you know.

"Dad," I said. "Before you go outside, I think you should know you only have one sock on."

Dad looked down at his foot. "Has anyone seen my other sock?"

"Try the roof," Mom said.

"Try Goofy's stomach," I said. "I think he ate it."

Goofy is our big white dog.

He is very open-minded about his diet.

Dad groaned. Then he went outside with his one bare foot. Followed by Max and Mom.

I checked on Hazel. She was talking to a blue dog on the TV screen.

Goofy was eating her cereal.

I went back to the junk drawer.

I picked up the *don't-you-dare* glue.

I imagined Mom saying, "Roscoe, don't you dare touch the *don't-you-dare* glue!"

I put the glue down.

I imagined my teacher saying, "Roscoe, what a wonderful helper you are! Thank you so much for the grown-up glue!"

Hazel came into the kitchen. She was wearing a paper crown.

Hazel's favorite games are Princess Dress-up, Mud Pie Picnic, and Let's Dress Up Roscoe Like a Princess and Make Him Eat Mud Pies.

". . . h, i, j, k, Ellen Emmo peed," Hazel sang.

She paused. "Who is Ellen Emmo?" she asked.

"They'll explain all that in kindergarten," I said.

I picked up the glue again.

Hazel's eyes got big. "That's the *don't-you-dare* glue!"

"It's for my teacher," I said. "Things are always breaking at school. Like yesterday, when I broke the pencil sharpener."

Sometimes I get a little carried away when I'm sharpening.

23

I put the glue in the bag of art supplies. Then I grabbed my Hero Guy backpack.

Hero Guy doesn't have his own TV show or anything.

Mom got him on sale at the mall.

"Hey, Roscoe," Max called. "Hurry up! The bus is coming! And you gotta come see something!"

I took Hazel's hand. I looked at the junk drawer one last time.

Maybe I should put the glue back, I thought.

After all, when you call something *don't-you-dare* glue, there's probably a good reason.

I could hear the bus driver honking.

Oh well, I thought.

It was just a harmless little bitty bottle of glue.

When Hazel and I got outside, I saw a big silver ladder leaning against the house.

Dad was holding it.

"Check it out!" Max exclaimed. "Mom's on the roof again!"

"Excellent," I said.

That is always a good way to start your day.

I yelled good-bye as I ran for the bus stop.

"See you at the open house!" Dad called.

Just then there was a big gust of wind.

The ladder fell with a crash.

Probably Mom would have yelled good-bye, too.

But she was too busy hanging from the roof.

6

The Secret Handshake

When I got to my classroom, my friends Gus and Emma ran over to say hello.

The first thing we did was our Secret Handshake.

Here is how it goes. In case you would like to try it.

1. Scream each other's names.

2. Wait for the teacher to say, "Inside voices, PLEASE!"

3. Do a high five.

4. Do a low five.

5. Stick out your tongue.

6. Get all serious and say, "How do you do, Mr. Riley?"

Of course, you would not say *Riley*, probably.

It would be pretty amazing if we had the same last name.

Emma pointed to my elbows. "Cool sparkle Band-Aids, Roscoe."

I mostly always have a Band-Aid on me somewhere.

Or a cast. Or a sling.

Mom says to think of it all as a fashion statement.

When I was four, I even had an eye patch.

The eye patch was black. Totally pirate.

"How'd you get the Band-Aids?" Gus asked.

"Racing my Hot Wheels car down the stairs," I said. "The Hot Wheels won."

"Household accidents are the most

common cause of injuries in children," said Emma.

Emma teaches me lots of interesting facts.

She was born in China. Her parents adopted her when she was a baby.

I wish I was born in China. Instead of just Kalamazoo.

Gus teaches me lots of useful things too.

Just last week he showed me how to make armpit farts.

"What's in the bag, Roscoe?" Emma asked.

"Art stuff for Ms. Diz," I said.

I opened the bag. Gus and Emma peeked inside.

"Cool head," Gus said.

"Her name was Drusilla," I said. "Before

I brain-surgeried her."

"Super-Mega-Gonzo Glue!" Gus said. "Whoa. My mom won't let me near that stuff!"

"Me either," said Emma.

"Me either," I said. "But I figured Ms. Diz could use it. For when we break stuff. Let's go show her what I brought."

Ms. Diz was busy stapling butterfly pictures to the bulletin board.

Ms. Diz isn't really her name.

But her real name is hard to say. It uses maybe half of the alphabet.

So she cut off the end for my class.

Maybe when I'm a grown-up, I'll be called Mr. Ri for short.

Or not.

I handed Ms. Diz the bag of art supplies. "This is for you," I said. "It's for the art

cupboard. There's special glue in there. And I even included a free head."

Ms. Diz frowned. "What *kind* of head, Roscoe?"

"Just a doll head." I smiled so she wouldn't worry.

Since Ms. Diz is new, she gets mixed up sometimes.

I try to help her out whenever I can.

After all, I was a kindergartner last year. So I already know everything there is to know about school.

For example, when Ms. Diz forgot the janitor's name, I remembered it was Mr. McGeely.

She had to call him when Gus threw up his ravioli after lunch.

Sometimes Ms. Diz looks pretty pooped by the end of the day.

I hope she doesn't decide to go into another line of work. My kindergarten teacher did that.

It wasn't my fault.

Probably.

Although I think maybe she got a little frustrated when I painted the class hamsters. Green. Because it was Saint Patrick's Day.

Hamsters like to look perky for the holidays.

Ms. Diz checked her watch. "Class!" she said in a loud voice.

Then she put a finger on her lips. That means SHHH.

"I know you're all excited about the open house today," said Ms. Diz. "We're going to have a dress rehearsal first thing this morning."

Dress rehearsal is when you practice with costumes and stuff.

It doesn't mean you have to wear a dress.

"Let's just hope things go a little better than they did yesterday," Ms. Diz said with a laugh. "I'm sure today we'll all be on our best behavior."

Poor old brand-new Ms. Diz.

I think maybe she forgot about our high spirits.

7

Mess Rehearsal

"First, I want all you bees to put on your antennae," said Ms. Diz.

Real bees use their head bobbles to smell and feel things.

But ours were just made of pipe cleaners and Styrofoam balls. With glitter on them.

They were attached to a plastic headband

thingie. Shaped like a great big upside-down U.

Last year the third graders used the bobbles for a play about butterflies.

So the headbands were a little stretched out by their gigantic third-grade heads.

When we were ready, Ms. Diz went to the music cupboard.

She handed each drummer two red tapping sticks.

We use the sticks for Music Time. They are our instruments.

Only really I would rather have a drum set.

Or a tuba.

"I know how much fun the sticks are, children," said Ms. Diz. "But as you may recall, some of you got a little carried away yesterday."

I think maybe she was looking at me.

But I wasn't the only one who got in stick trouble.

Gus was the one who started the pretend sword fight.

I was Not Guilty.

Mostly.

"Our rhythm section sits in the chairs," said Ms. Diz. "Nice and still."

That was me. And Gus. And Dewan and Maria and Coco.

"All the other bees in the back row," said Ms. Diz. "Standing up nice and tall."

We got into our places.

Bees and bee drummers.

Bobbles and sticks.

We were ready for action.

"Okay, let's sing nice and clear," said Ms. Diz. "And no poking with the sticks."

"How about swords?" Dewan asked.

"No swords," said Ms. Diz.

"How about death rays?" Gus asked.

"No death rays," said Ms. Diz. "When I count to three, start singing!"

Here is how our bee song goes:

Buzzy bees, fuzzy bees,
Look at us fly!
Bees are the best bugs!
You want to know why?
We make our own honey
and soar in the sky.
Can you do what we do?
We dare you to try!

"Great job!" said Ms. Diz when we were done. "Roscoe, you sound especially wonderful. But we need to hear the other kids too."

"He's blowing out my eardrums, Ms. Diz," Coco complained.

"My head bobbles keep falling off!" Wyatt said.

Ms. Diz took a deep breath.

"I know the antennae don't fit very well, children. Just do the best you can. Let's try the song one more time. This time, let me hear those sticks pounding out the rhythm!"

We sang again. I was not so loud this time.

But if you ask me, they were missing out.

"Better," said Ms. Diz when we were done.

"My bobbles keep falling in my eyes!" Hassan said.

"Oh, dear," said Ms. Diz. "Maybe we should just forget about the antennae."

"But we have to have bobbles!" Coco cried. "Otherwise how will our parents know we're bees?"

"You make a good point, Coco. Hassan, bring me your antennae," said Ms. Diz. "Maybe I can tighten them up a little."

While Ms. Diz worked on Hassan's bobbles, Maria started tapping her sticks.

Dewan tapped along.

Gus tapped too.

On my head.

"Children," said Ms. Diz. She was still trying to fix Hassan's bobbles. "No tapping, please."

We sat and waited. While we sat there, I came up with a new invention.

I put the rhythm sticks in my mouth.

I made them point straight down.

Ta-da! Walrus teeth!

I think when I grow up I may be a famous inventor.

Or else an ice cream truck driver.

Dewan and Gus laughed at my walrus teeth.

Maria put her sticks on her head. She looked just like an alien.

Even more people laughed.

Gus put his sticks up his nose.

He just looked gross.

Pretty soon we were all tapping and laughing and being walruses and aliens.

Except Gus.

He just kept the sticks in his nose.

"Children!" said Ms. Diz loudly.

But we couldn't hear her very well.

What with all the tapping and laughing.

Gus held up one of his nose sticks. "I challenge you to a duel!" he cried.

"Yuck," said Coco.

I jumped up on my chair.

So did Gus.

You can't sword-fight sitting down.

We sort of forgot about the no-sword-fighting rule.

"Roscoe!!! Gus!!! Children!!!" Ms. Diz held up her hand and put a finger to her lips. "Quiet down NOW!"

We got very quiet.

Gus and I froze on our chairs.

Ms. Diz pointed to the doorway.

Mr. Goosegarden was standing there.

He is the principal. That is the big boss of the school.

He is mostly nice.

Unless you've been Making Bad Choices.

Then you have to sit in his office and think about your behavior.

When that happens, Mr. Goosegarden wears his I-mean-business face.

And right now, Mr. Goosegarden had on his I-REALLY-mean-business face.

8

How to Speak Teacher

"Children," said Mr. Goosegarden. "I certainly hope you won't disappoint your parents with this kind of rowdy behavior at the open house."

Coco raised her hand.

"Roscoe started it, Mr. Goosegarden," she said. "He made walrus teeth."

Coco was not really being helpful.

If you ask me.

"I'm sure Roscoe will remember that walrus teeth are not appropriate," said Mr. Goosegarden. "And that chairs are for sitting. Not sword fighting."

He winked at me.

Mr. Goosegarden and I go way back.

"Sorry," I said. "I didn't know there was a no-walrus-teeth rule."

"That's okay, Roscoe," said Mr. Goosegarden. "I know you will come through this afternoon."

He smiled at Ms. Diz. "Don't worry," he said. "The first year of teaching is always the hardest."

Mr. Goosegarden waved good-bye. The door closed behind him.

Ms. Diz sighed.

She looked at the clock on the wall. "It's way past time for reading groups.

Let's take off the head bobbles. . . . I mean the *antennae*. Just do the best you can this afternoon."

She sounded sort of worn-out.

I felt bad about the walrus-teeth incident.

Like I said before, kids have so many rules to remember!

There are a gazillion things we are not supposed to do.

Who knew making walrus teeth was one of them?

. . .

After we put away the bobbles and sticks, we sat at tables for reading groups.

Reading is fun. But it can be very hard work.

You can get pretty thirsty trying to make those letters into words.

After I read four whole sentences,

I went to the water fountain to get a drink.

The fountain is next to the art cupboard.

Just then, Mr. Frisbee came in. He is a kindergarten teacher.

"May I borrow some chalk?" Mr. Frisbee asked Ms. Diz.

"Sure," said Ms. Diz. She opened the art cupboard. I could see the art supplies I'd brought.

Including Drucilla's head.

And the *don't-you-dare* glue.

Ms. Diz gave Mr. Frisbee a fresh box of chalk. "Here you go," she said.

"How was the dress rehearsal?" Mr. Frisbee asked.

Ms. Diz whispered something I couldn't hear.

Then she laughed. "At this rate, I'll be

looking for another job soon!"

They both laughed.

But I was pretty sure it was worried laughing.

Maybe you are wondering how I could tell.

After all, teachers can be confusing.

Not as confusing as parents.

But still. Sometimes teachers have trouble expressing themselves.

Fortunately, I have served in preschool and kindergarten already.

Also Mommy and Me Music.

And Gymborama.

And my clay class, Pots for Tots.

So I am happy to explain teacher stuff to you.

Here is my Goof-Proof Roscoe Riley Teacher Translator:

It's pretty easy to understand teachers.
Once you get the hang of it.

I'm still working on figuring out how to speak Parent, though.

I thought about what Ms. Diz had said to Mr. Frisbee. *At this rate, I'll be looking for another job soon.*

What if Mr. Goosegarden fired Ms. Diz? Just because of our rowdy behavior?

That would be awful.

After all, Ms. Diz is a great teacher.

Even if she is just a beginner.

Then I thought about my kindergarten teacher from last year.

The one who changed jobs after I painted the hamsters.

She works at an office now.

With no kids in it.

And no green hamsters.

How boring is that?

I could not let such a horrible thing happen to Ms. Diz.

9

Roscoe to the Rescue

Right after recess, it was time to get ready
for the open house.

Ms. Diz and the room mothers set out
chocolate chip cookies and cakes and pies
on a big table.

And napkins and juice.

Those cookies looked DELICIOUS.

But I was too worried about the bee song to think about those delicious, chewy, chocolaty, melt-in-my-mouth cookies.

Well, *almost* too worried.

Ms. Diz arranged the chairs. Then she set out the sticks and the head bobbles on the counter.

"Your parents will be here in just a few minutes, children," she said. "Check all the activity centers to be sure everything is nice and clean."

"Ms. Diz?" called one of the room mothers. "Do you have any name tags?"

"I think I have some in the art cupboard," said Ms. Diz.

She opened the cupboard doors. "Nope. No name tags. Let me see if they have any in the office. Children, I'll be right back. Roscoe, why don't you pass out the antennae? Dewan, you hand out the sticks. But no funny business. The rest of you finish cleaning up."

Ms. Diz rushed out the door.

The art cupboard doors were still open.

I could see the *don't-you-dare* glue I'd brought.

And just then I had a Super-Mega-Gonzo idea.

I went over to the cupboard.

All the kids were busy cleaning up blocks and puzzle pieces and crayons.

The room mothers were not paying attention to me, either.

They were busy mopping up a juice spill. It was caused by a flying LEGO.

I picked up one of the head bobbles on the counter.

I reached for the *don't-you-dare* glue.

I tried to read the label.

It took a LOT of work to read it.

Bonds instantly and permanently, it said. *Glues wood, metal, glass, and paper.*

The label did not mention head bobbles.

I opened the glue.

I put a little on the headband.

And I popped those bobbles on my head.

I waited a few seconds.

Then I wiggled my head.

The bobbles stayed on!

Nice and tight. Just like real bee bobbles.

Perfect.

I put a few drops of glue on all the other bobbles.

Then I slipped the tube of glue into my pocket.

One by one, I passed out bobbles to all the kids.

Hassan tried on his bobbles.

He didn't notice the little drops of *don't-you-dare* glue.

"Hey," said Hassan. He shook his head. "Weird. My bobbles are staying on!"

"So are mine," Maria said. "Ms. Diz must have fixed them."

I handed bobbles to Gus and Dewan.

They were playing swords again.

"Gus!" I said. "No swords! This open house has got to be perfect."

"They're not swords," he said. "They're lightsabers."

"Here," I said. I put the bobbles on his head.

And gave the last pair to Dewan, who put them on.

"Hey," said Dewan. "My bobbles aren't bobbling!"

Mission accomplished, I thought.

Roscoe to the rescue!

10

Bee-having

Ms. Diz came back with the name tags.

She was not happy to see Gus and Dewan playing swords again.

"Drummers, settle down," she said firmly.

"My bobbles are staying on, Ms. Diz," Maria reported.

"And so are mine," said Coco.

Ms. Diz looked surprised. "Hmm," she

said. "That's good news."

Just then Coco's mom and dad arrived. "Smile, everyone!" said her mom. "We're recording!"

Coco's dad was holding a silver camcorder.

All the other moms and dads began to come in.

They smiled and talked and waved and shook hands.

While Ms. Diz was busy saying hello, Gus pointed his stick at Dewan. "I am Zorro!" he yelled.

"I am Darth Vader!" cried Dewan.

"Duel to the death!" Gus shouted.

They were going to have a hard time sitting still for the bee song, I thought.

And then I had another Super-Mega-Gonzo idea.

Sometimes my brain amazes me.

I went over to the drummer chairs.

I looked around. Nobody was watching me. And Mom and Dad weren't there yet.

I pulled out the *don't-you-dare* glue. And I put a few drops on each chair seat.

I smiled a proud smile.

The bee song would go perfectly.

Ms. Diz would keep her job.

And all because of me.

"Roscoe! Hello, Pumpkin!" someone called.

It was Mom.

She was carrying her banana-avocado-raisin cream pie.

It is not really okay for moms to call you "Pumpkin" in front of your classmates.

But that's all right. Sometimes parents forget to follow the rules too.

My dad was right behind her.

He was carrying Hazel.

Hazel only goes to preschool half a day.

Little kids have it so easy.

"What's on Roscoe's head, Mommy?" Hazel asked.

"These are my bee bobbles," I said proudly.

I wiggled my head. They stayed put.

I am a genius, I thought.

Ms. Diz clapped her hands and put a finger to her lips.

"Parents, please find a seat. We have an exciting performance planned for you!"

All the moms and dads sat down.

They had to squish into our little bitty chairs.

They looked pretty silly.

I was glad no one tried to sit in the chairs I'd glued.

"Places, everyone," said Ms. Diz.

The bees lined up.

The bee drummers sat down.

Right on the glue.

All except Gus.

"There's something on my chair," he complained.

"Probably your own nose goo," said Coco.

"Gus," said Ms. Diz. "Please sit down."

Gus sighed. He sat down with a plop.

"As you may know, we've been studying insects these past few weeks," Ms. Diz said.

Suddenly Mr. Goosegarden appeared in the doorway.

"Hello, parents!" he said. "I'm just passing through. Didn't want to miss hearing my favorite beehive perform!"

Mr. Goosegarden looked at all of us.

One eyebrow went up.

Just like my dad's.

I wonder if there's a school where they learn that eyebrow move.

Ms. Diz made a noise with her throat. Her face was a little pink.

Or maybe green.

I think that's called stage fright.

"As I was saying," she said. "We've

been learning about insects. Especially bees. And now we have a song we'd like to perform for you."

Hazel made a buzzing sound.

All the parents laughed.

Everyone thinks she's adorable.

It's disgusting.

"All right, children," said Ms. Diz. She made her voice a whisper. "We are going to do this just right this time!"

She looked over at the drummers.

Even Gus was sitting perfectly still.

Not that he had a choice.

"One, two, three!" said Ms. Diz.

We all sang loud and clear. And pounded nice and steady.

When we were done, the parents cheered and clapped.

Someone even whistled.

"Bravo!" a dad yelled.

Coco's mom wiped tears from her eyes.

"Can we have cookies now?" asked Hazel.

Ms. Diz looked very happy.

And she wasn't pink or green anymore.

Mr. Goosegarden grinned. "Children, I knew you'd come through. That was just perfect. I must say that I loved the way you BEE-haved."

Everyone laughed at his bee joke.

Because you have to laugh when it's the principal.

Mr. Goosegarden gave Ms. Diz a thumbs-up sign.

That means GOOD JOB.

Also YOU WON'T HAVE TO GO WORK IN A BORING, HAMSTER-FREE OFFICE.

He gave us all a big wave.

And then he left.

I couldn't stop smiling. Everything had gone perfectly.

Thanks to me.

And a little bit of *don't-you-dare* glue.

"All right, everybody," said Ms. Diz. "Hand me your antennae and your sticks. And line up with your parents for dessert."

All the kids clapped and cheered.

Then everybody pulled off their head bobbles.

At least, everybody *tried* to pull off their head bobbles.

"Ouch!" Emma cried.

"The bobbles won't come off!" Dewan shouted.

"My hairs are pulling!" Gus yelled.

"MY BOBBLES ARE STUCK!!!" Coco screamed.

Everybody looked at me.

Their faces were kind of surprised.

Then mad.

Then REALLY mad.

It seemed like maybe a good time for me to go to the bathroom.

But when I tried to get up, my chair came with me.

11

Uh-Oh

I yanked on that chair.

I tugged.

I pulled.

I whirled around like Goofy chasing his tail.

Gus and Dewan and Coco and Maria tried to get up too.

But those chairs were stuck to our clothes.

Permanently.

Just like the glue label had promised.

"Uh-oh," I said. Real softly.

No one heard me except Gus.

All the kids were too busy screaming about their bobbles.

And running around like crazy people.

Parents were dashing over to see what all the fuss was about.

Coco's dad was recording the whole mess.

And Ms. Diz looked a little like she might faint.

If you asked me, they were getting a little carried away about the head bobbles.

I mean, really, SOME of us had more important problems.

Like butt chairs.

"Roscoe," Gus said. "How come you said 'Uh-oh'? Did you do something?"

"The *don't-you-dare* glue," I whispered.

"I sort of dared."

"Whoa." Gus wiggled the chair attached

to his rear end. "That is SOME glue."

"I'm doomed," I said.

"Totally," Gus said.

Emma ran over to me. She was yanking on her head bobbles.

Just like everyone else.

"Roscoe," she said, "did you use the *don't-you-dare* glue on the bobbles?"

That Emma!

She knows me so well.

"ROSCOE RILEY!" Coco yelled. "THIS IS ALL YOUR FAULT! YOU ARE THE ONE WHO HANDED OUT THE BOBBLES!"

"Mommy!" Hazel said. "Is Roscoe going to time-out?"

"Roscoe?" Ms. Diz said.

"Roscoe?" said Mom.

"Roscoe?" said Dad.

I could hardly hear them.

What with all the screaming.

"Roscoe?" Ms. Diz said again. Louder this time. "Is there something you'd like to tell us?"

"What have you done to my Coco's beautiful head?" Coco's mom screamed.

I started to answer.

But just then Coco ran by.

Actually, Coco and her chair ran by.

"GET IT OFF OF ME!" she screeched.

That girl really has a great pair of lungs.

I tried to stop her so I could explain everything.

Only I sort of missed and grabbed one of her chair legs instead.

Coco lost her balance.

She tripped.

She did a way cool air somersault.

Right onto the dessert table.

All those beautiful desserts went flying.

Also Mom's horrible banana-avocado-raisin cream pie.

I watched that pie float through the air.

It was like a slow-motion movie.

Higher and higher.

Twirling and swirling.

A deadly missile made of bananas and avocados and raisins.

And it was heading straight for poor Ms. Diz.

I knew what I had to do.

After all the trouble I'd caused, I had to save my teacher.

I leaped into the air.

Which isn't easy to do when you have a chair attached to your butt.

SPLAT!!!!

That pie landed right in my face.

A direct hit.

Pie in my hair. On my clothes. On my bobbles.

I lay on the floor.

Chair glued to me.

Pie covering me.

Kids screaming.

Parents yelling.

But Ms. Diz was safe.

And you know, that pie really wasn't half bad.

12

Holes in Our Heads

Ms. Diz and the parents had to use scissors to cut us off our chairs.

That part was a little embarrassing.

Plus we had to borrow clothes from the lost-and-found box.

I had to wear pink bunny pants.

That part was WAY embarrassing.

They had to cut off our bobbles too.

We all lost a little hair.

Because of the glue situation.

Some of the kids were not too happy about the holes in their heads.

But I reminded them that their hair would grow back before they knew it.

I had to have a long talk with Ms. Diz and Mom and Dad.

When I explained to Ms. Diz how I was trying to save her job, she gave me a hug.

That is Teacher for *I forgive you, kiddo*.

She made me promise that next time I'd ask first before I tried to save her.

And to never, ever, ever touch *don't-you-dare* glue again.

She also said she loved her job.

And that Mr. Goosegarden would think the whole glue story was funny. Someday.

Like I said.

Ms. Diz is a great teacher.

Even if she is just a beginner.

13

Good-Bye from Time-Out

So now you know why I'm in time-out.

Actually, Mom and Dad were really proud of me for trying to help Ms. Diz.

They just didn't like the part where I took the *don't-you-dare* glue out of the drawer to begin with.

Now that I think about it, I can see

their point.

That glue is way sticky.

Anyway, thank you for hanging out with me.

It's been nice to have some company.

Here come Mom and Dad now.

I'm going to tell them again how sorry I am.

And then maybe we'll go to the barber shop to fix my bald spots.

Now I know how my dad feels.

But first we'll have a big hug.

That's the best part of time-out.

10 WAY COOL THINGS THAT SOMEBODY SHOULD INVENT

by Me, Roscoe Riley

1. Chocolate spaghetti

2. A water slide for my bathtub

3. Popcorn-flavored bubble gum

4. Invisible spray (for broccoli and other emergencies)

5. Trampoline floors at school

6. Robots that pick up dirty socks

7. Remote controls with a MUTE button for little sisters

8. Remote controls with a MUTE button for big brothers

9. One-size-fits-all head bobbles

10. Super-Mega-Gonzo Glue Remover

Turn the page for a
super-special sneak peek
at MY next adventure!

ROSCOE RILEY
Rules #2

Never Swipe
a Bully's Bear

Here's how the trouble starts:

I wouldn't be stuck here in time-out if I'd just listened to my big brother.

And believe me, I hardly ever say that.

It started the other day. I was packing Hamilton into my backpack.

So he could go to school with me. Just like always.

Max saw me. "No pigs allowed at school, Roscoe," he said.

I ignored him.

Because number one, that isn't a rule.

Unless the pig is the real kind.

And number two, when a little brother ignores a big brother, it drives the big brother crazy.

Max was eating Cheerios. He threw one at my head. "You're in first grade now," he said. "And first graders do NOT take stuffed animals to school."

I picked the Cheerio out of my hair.

Then I ate it.

That also drives big brothers crazy.

"Hamilton always comes with me," I said.

Mom ran into the kitchen. "Has anyone seen Hazel's Cinderella toothbrush?"

Hazel is my little sister. She has a thing about princesses. Also mud.

"The point is, stuffed animals are for babies," Max said.

"Max!" Mom said. "What are you talking about?"

"Roscoe's taking that stinkpot Bacon to school," Max said.

"That isn't his name," I said.

"Ham," Max said.

"Ham-ILTON," I said.

"It would be totally embarrassing if anyone sees you with that thing," Max said. "I'd be humiliated!"

"You are in fourth grade," Mom said. "Roscoe's in first. How is he going to humiliate you?"

Max shook his head. "I'm sorry, Mom," he said, "but you know nothing about the real world. People will talk."

"That pig is Roscoe's best friend," Mom said. "And as long as it's okay with his teacher, he may take Bacon—I mean

Hamilton—to school."

"Besides, nobody knows he's there," I pointed out. "'Cause he stays in my backpack. Only Emma and Gus know about him. And Ms. Diz."

Ms. Diz is my teacher. And Emma and Gus are my best buddies.

Max made a pig-snort sound.

I snorted back. Twice.

Let me tell you, dealing with big brothers is an art.

"I'm bringing Hamilton," I said. "And that's that."

The thing is, I've had Hamilton forever.

My Great-aunt Hilda sent him to me on my first birthday.

She has a pig farm in North Carolina.

Great-aunt Hilda says pigs are very intelligent and lovable.

Sort of like snorting dogs.

I can't sleep without Hamilton.

When I was little, he kept away monsters and fire-breathing dragons.

When I got bigger, he kept away black widow spiders and grizzly bears.

He is my guard pig.

"Guys!" Dad called. "Hustle! It's almost time for the bus!"

Max ran to get his backpack. Mom ran to find Hazel's toothbrush.

I sat in the kitchen and stared at Hamilton.

I put him on the counter.

What if Max was right?

I was getting awfully old.

I mean, I had a loose tooth. That's WAY old.

Hamilton looked worried, like he might start to cry.

I could see this was very hard for him.

"Okay, buddy, you can come," I said.

I smushed Hamilton into the very bottom of my backpack.

I left the zipper open a little. So he could breathe.

Max was crazy. Nobody would bug me about Hamilton.

Because nobody knew about him. Except Ms. Diz and Emma and Gus.

I peeked into my backpack.

"Hamilton," I said. "You can come to school with me forever. Even when I'm a fourth grader."

Katherine Applegate has never glued anyone to a chair (at least, that's what she claims).

She is the author of lots of books for kids and lives in Chapel Hill, North Carolina, with her two terrific kids, two wacky dogs, two cranky cats, two tubby guinea pigs, and one patient husband. She has not been in time-out in quite a while, but her dog Goofy was recently sent there for breaking rule #132: Never eat a hula hoop.